A Note to Parents

For many children, learning math is difficult and "I hate math!" is their first response — to which many parents silently add "Me, too!" Children often see adults comfortably reading and writing, but they rarely have such models for mathematics. And math fear can be catching!

The easy-to-read stories in this ***Hello Math*** series were written to give children a positive introduction to mathematics, and parents a pleasurable re-acquaintance with a subject that is important to everyone's life. ***Hello Math*** stories make mathematical ideas accessible, interesting, and fun for children. The activities and suggestions at the end of each book provide parents with a hands-on approach to help children develop mathematical interest and confidence.

Enjoy the mathematics!
• Give your child a chance to retell the story. The more familiar children are with the story, the more they will understand its mathematical concepts.
• Use the colorful illustrations to help children "hear and see" the math at work in the story.
• Treat the math activities as games to be played for fun. Follow your child's lead. Spend time on those activities that engage your child's interest and curiosity.
• Activities, especially ones using physical materials, help make abstract mathematical ideas concrete.

Learning is a messy process. Learning about math calls for children to become immersed in lively experiences that help them make sense of mathematical concepts and symbols.

Although learning about numbers is basic to math, other ideas, such as identifying shapes and patterns, measuring, collecting and interpreting data, reasoning logically, and thinking about chance, are also important. By reading these stories and having fun with the activities, you will help your child enthusiastically say "***Hello, Math***," instead of "I hate math."

ducator
thematics! Book

For my sisters, Karen and Ellen,
who shared their rooms
— J.R.

For Cecilia and Celeste
—C.O.

Library of Congress Cataloging-in-Publication Data

Rocklin, Joanne.
Not enough room! / by Joanne Rocklin; math activities by Marilyn Burns; illustrated by Cristina Ong.
p. cm. — (Hello math reader. Level 2)
Summary: When two sisters have to move into the same room, they use tape to divide the room into different shapes so that each one can have her own space. Includes related activities.
ISBN 0-590-39962-4
[1. Sisters—Fiction. 2. Shape—Fiction. 3. Stories in rhyme.]
I. Burns, Marilyn. II. Ong, Cristina, ill. III. Title. IV. Series
PZ8.3.R595No 1998
[E]—dc21 97-12853
CIP
AC

12 11 10 9 8 7 6 5 4 3 2 8 9/9 0/0 01 02

Printed in the U.S.A. 24

First Scholastic printing, January 1998

by Joanne Rocklin
Illustrated by Cristina Ong
Math Activities by Marilyn Burns

Hello Math Reader — Level 2

SCHOLASTIC INC.
New York Toronto London Auckland Sydney

Once I had my own room.
So did my sister Kris.
We had two square rooms
that looked like this:

WINDOW
DOOR
PAT'S ROOM

We had lots of space
for our beds and our chairs,
our clothes and our books,
and our big stuffed bears.

But then Mom said,
“Baby’s coming soon.
Kris and Pat,
you must share Pat’s room.”

"Oh, no!" cried my sister.
"I won't share with Pat.
I want my own room
and that is that!"

"Look at this drawing,"
I said to Kris.
"Your very own room will
look like this.
A rectangular room
is a very good shape.
We can make your room
with sticky tape."

WINDOW
PAT'S ROOM
TAPE
KRIS'S ROOM
DOOR

"I'll give it a try,"
my sister said.
So that day she moved
her books and her bed,
her clothes and her chair,
and her big stuffed bear
into that room with a
rectangular shape
that we made by using sticky tape.

But my rectangular room
seemed kind of small.
Maybe a triangular room
was the best shape of all.

"We must move again,"
I said to Kris.
"We can make two rooms
that look like this."

So we moved our beds
and we moved our chairs,
our clothes and our books,
and our big stuffed bears
into two rooms with a
triangular shape that we
made by using sticky tape.

"We must move back!"
I said to Kris.
"The corners are small
in a room like this!"

So we moved things here
and we moved things there,
back to those two
rectangular rooms
inside one big square.

WINDOW
PAT'S ROOM
TAPE
KRIS'S ROOM
DOOR

"I need some rest!"
my sister said.
She flopped right down
on her comfortable bed.

"Oh, no!" I said.
"We must move once more.
You need a window
and I need a door!"

“Just one more time,”
I said to Kris.
“We need rectangular rooms
that look like this. ”

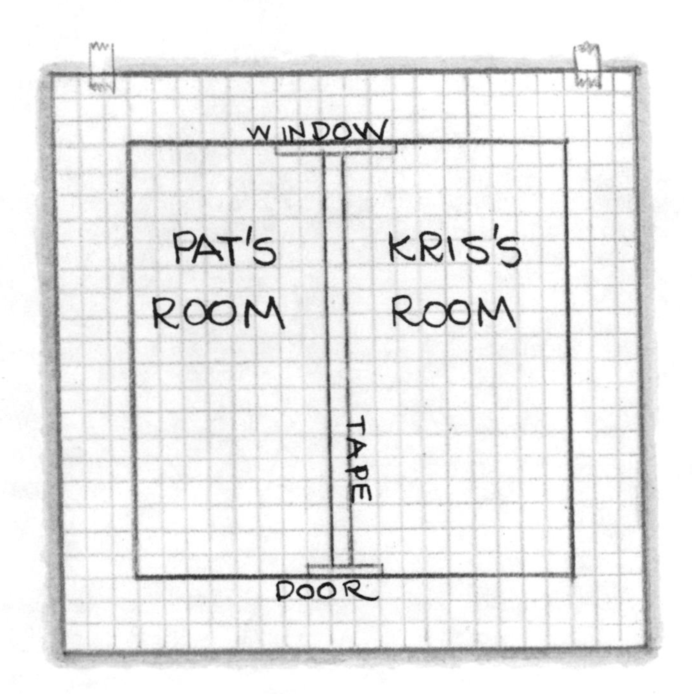

So we moved our beds,
our books and our chairs,
our clothes and our toys,
and our big stuffed bears
into the rooms of rectangular shape
that we made by using sticky tape.

My sister said,
"Now, listen, Pat!
No more moving
and that is that!"

But one day the baby
pulled up the tape,
and we forgot all about each
rectangular shape.

And soon after that, Mom said,
"Girls, close your eyes!
I have got a terrific surprise!"

Now my sister and I
never, ever need tape,
because our big square room
is the very best shape!

• About the Activities •

All children have faced the problem of sharing something fairly. This story builds on children's familiarity with sharing and presents them with a situation that calls for thinking about geometry. Kris and Pat have to decide how to divide a square room so that each of them is satisfied with her half.

The problem presented in the story gives children the opportunity to think about how a square might be divided in half creating two triangles or two rectangles. An important part of studying geometry in the elementary grades is for children to learn how shapes can be divided into other shapes and how shapes can be put together to make different shapes.

The activities that follow build on the story and suggest more ways of working with squares and other shapes. Since geometry is such a visual area of mathematics, be prepared with paper, pencil, and scissors to use as you explore the math concepts. Have fun getting in shape with geometry!

—Marilyn Burns

You'll find tips and suggestions for guiding the activities whenever you see a box like this!

Retelling the Story

Kris and Pat had a problem. They had to figure out how to share one square room.

Pat first suggested that they use sticky tape to divide the room into two rectangular rooms. But the rooms seemed too small.

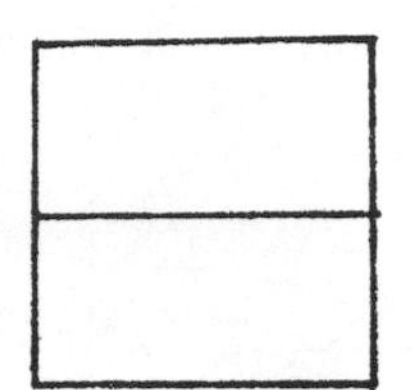

Then Pat suggested that they use sticky tape to divide the room into two triangular rooms. But the corners seemed too small.

The sisters went back to their first solution of two rectangular rooms, but then moved one last time. This time they split the square room in the other direction to divide the room into two rectangular rooms again.

Which way do you think made the most sense for Kris and Pat to divide the room?

More Halves of Squares

Kris and Pat divided their square room either into two triangles or into two rectangles. But there are other ways to divide a square so the two halves are the same shape and size. Here's one way:

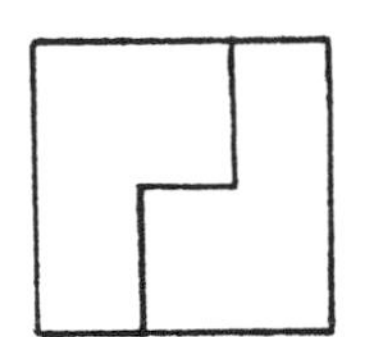

And there are ways to divide a square into halves that are not the same shape! Here's one of those ways:

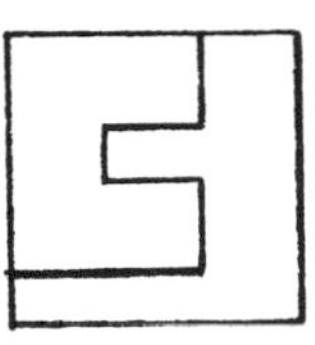

Trace the square below and try to find a different way to divide it in half. Trace more squares and look for other ways to divide them into halves.

Exploring with Triangles

You can make many different shapes by putting other shapes together. Try doing this with triangles. Draw a square and cut it into two triangles.

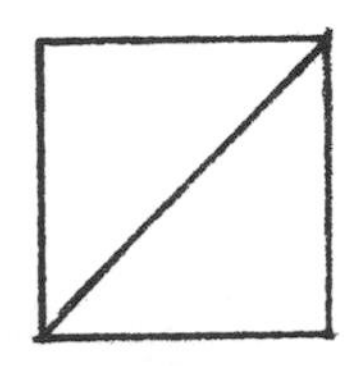

Put the triangles together so that two of the same length sides are matching. You can make three shapes—a square, a triangle, and a parallelogram.

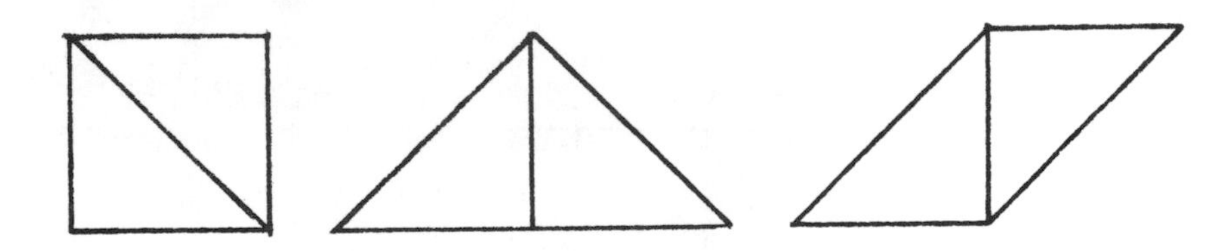

Now draw another square the same size and cut out two more triangles. Put these with the other triangles so you have four altogether. (Be sure they are all the same size and shape.) Find different ways to put the four triangles together. Be sure to follow the rule that the same length sides must match. Here are just two possible shapes you can make. (There are 12 more).

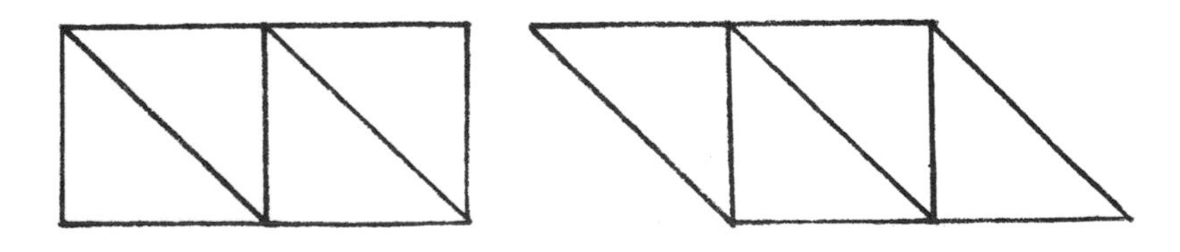

Geometry Words

Kris and Pat had to share a room that was shaped like a square. When they first divided their room, they put sticky tape down the middle parallel to two sides of the square. Each part was shaped like a rectangle. Then they tried another way and divided their room into two triangular shapes by putting sticky tape from corner to corner, right on the diagonal of their room.

Figure out which of these words — square, parallel, rectangle, triangle, or diagonal — answers the riddles below.

1. What's the name of a line segment that goes from one corner of a rectangle to the opposite corner?

2. What's the name of a shape that has three straight sides and three corners?

3. What's the name of a shape that has four straight sides and all square corners?

4. What's the name of a shape that has four straight sides of the same length, and all square corners?

5. When two lines go in the same direction so they won't ever cross, what are they called?

Answers:
1. diagonal 2. triangle 3. rectangle or square
4. square (but *not* a rectangle!) 5. parallel

Crazy Geometry

Have you ever heard of a crazy quilt? It's a quilt that is made by putting together lots of differently shaped pieces of material of many colors and patterns. Cut out about 20 geometric shapes—triangles, squares, rectangles, parallelograms, etc., and see if you can piece them together. Cutting your geometric shapes out of different kinds of wrapping paper makes a pretty quilt.